THE MULTI-COLORED *Flower*

By Daphne Stockman

Copyright © 2015 by Daphne Stockman . 695515
Library of Congress Control Number: 2015919785

ISBN: Softcover 978-1-5144-3080-4
      EBook   978-1-514-43081-1

All rights reserved. No part of this book may be reproduced or transmitted in any form or by any means, electronic or mechanical, including photocopying, recording, or by any information storage and retrieval system, without permission in writing from the copyright owner.

This is a work of fiction. Names, characters, places and incidents either are the product of the author's imagination or are used fictitiously, and any resemblance to any actual persons, living or dead, events, or locales is entirely coincidental.

Print information available on the last page

Rev. date: 1/20/2016

To order additional copies of this book, contact:
Xlibris
1-888-795-4274
www.Xlibris.com
Orders@Xlibris.com

MULTI-COLORED FLOWER

Contents:

1. Cover page
2. Introduction
3. A multi-colored flower
4. Petals from the multi-colored flower:

   1. Claypots-We are one in the Spirit
   2. We are one in the Spirit
   3. Petals of Gold

5. Illusion Vs Reality
6. A Paradox ?
7. Virtues and Values
8. Inner Freedom and Integrity
9. Build Bridges not Walls
10. The Salad Bowl: Multiculturalism-Assimilation towards Integration.

INTRODUCTION:

HERALDING THE WIND OF CHANGE

I would like to quote from a very beautiful song by the Scorpions called "The Wind of Change"

"The world is closing in, and did you ever think that we could be so close, like brothers (and sisters...added by me) The future is in the air, can feel it everywhere blowing with the wind of change. Take me to the magic of the moment on a glory night where the children of tomorrow dream and wait in the wind of change. Walking down the street and distant memories are buried in the past forever. I follow them in this world down to world's end listening to the wind of change. The wind of change blows straight into the face of time like a storm wind bringing rain the freedom bells for peace of mind, letting me to sing what my guitar wants to say"

2016 A LEAP YEAR TO REVOLUTIONARY CHANGE

As we enter 2016 the keyword around us seems to be CHANGE. The process of drastic change envelops the globe. However 'change' must and will only be for the better, if there is a 'personal revolution' within individuals. This book : Multi-colored Flower is speaking of change and the author is happy to publish it in the Leap Year.

In a personal revolution YOU are your own enemy and conquest of self is the goal.

As we enter 2016 we need to turn a corner and take a new road to a new direction. We must be prepared to break the bonds of past slavery and enter a "freedom of spirit" to be who we truly are. Our revolution calls for smashing destructive idols and images and gaining a new vision of the person one is called to become. It calls for waking up and coming alive to stop 'drift'. It means grabbing the oars and rowing with a purpose. It calls for overcoming the fear and failure complex by Faith in Someone greater than you. This revolution will be a Declaration of Freedom from all that would drag one down to reaching for all that will lift one up.

This is the Challenge for the whole world. This is the LEAP we can take

A MULTI-COLOURED FLOWER

(A Parable)

This is a story about a garden of flowers which needed to breathe its sweet fragrance in the morn, adding to the ruddy colors of the dawn. There were roses and daffodils, dhalias and lotus, cherry blossoms and gardenia, primroses and daisies. There were dandelions and buttercups as well as lilies and violets.

Each had its own bed and bloomed ever so perfectly at the loving and caring hands of the gardener who even spoke to them..

However they grew in separate beds, focused on how beautiful their appearance ought to be for people to admire. This situation caused much dissatisfaction among the flowers as the expectations and pride of each bed of flowers rose to a point of envy..

Though rooted in fertile soil and flowering with the right combination of rain and sun and nurtured by the gardener, some wanted to be like the others. For example, the dandelions took pleasure in criticizing the roses and the lotus wanted to be like the lilies, so there was much unhappiness in this garden. Each did not yet understand the uniqueness and the wonderful gift it was to the other. The air was so vitiated with negative energy that the atmosphere and elements were affected.

Powerless against the strong winds that blew destructively, sometimes even for days, the petals of the flowers flew all around . They were swept and thrown into the stream at the side of the garden, where they danced upon the waters like a kaleidoscope of colors till they faded and drowned.

The bees that visited the flowers everyday could not sit on some of them to extract pollen as it was bitter to taste and, in some cases, there was no pollen to extract. This caused a greater rift among the flowers as they calculated their success from the number of bees that visited.

Was the garden's beauty only on the outside? Why this inner conflict? Why this envy and dissatisfaction ?

As the storm came and the winds blew stronger the dandelion seeds were scattered and some fell on the flower beds, grew wildly hampering the growth of the flowers.

The gardener was very sad and disturbed as the situation became worse and some

flower plants died. More rain came down in torrents and the garden was swamped. Where had all the flowers gone?

What grew in such lovely colorful profusion was destroyed by bitterness, the spreading of negativity and domination of forceful elements. Love and beauty had disappeared.

Many weeks passed before the ground dried and the gardener took a lot of pain to restore the soil to its former richness and vigor. He then got ready to replant the flower seeds.

One night the new and young flower seeds got together and made a plan. When the gardener came the next morning they told him "Sir, we do not want to be planted separately . Every time we see our petals floating in the water we cry with pain. We have a plan"

The good gardener asked "What is your plan?" They said "While we wish to be ourselves roses, lilies and so on, we want to give a petal or two each to form a multi-colored flower which will remind us that we are one and united."

The gardener thought this was a good idea and went about devising a way to make this beautiful multi-colored flower in which every flower would participate.

At last the gardener was able to make this wonder with the help of the flower seeds themselves. The multi-colored flower was highly admired by everyone.

Was there a place for the dandelion? Surely, the dandelion is also very beautiful, as it grows through a process to make a pattern. The gardener put it in a separate bed and it contributed some of its beautiful yellow flowers . Later dandelions were taken for medicinal and commercial uses by companies. They had a role indeed!

To avoid the floods the level of the garden was raised. The garden regained its splendor. Children and elderly, youth and families found such peace and beauty in the scene, so much of brightness and laughter in the sunny landscape, such music in the song of the birds, such freedom in the flight of the crows and so much joy for all.

This is a parable but the story I give below is the multi-colored flower in reality.

Part II

On July 2nd 1959, the first multi-colored flower came into being at a school in Kurseong, India

A pioneering group of 5 boys, all of different communities in India, formed the

God's Leaders Squad. It was at the time when India was grappling with destructive forces in the hills of West Bengal.

In the preamble of the original Constitution they adopted to work in the name of God and for his glory to prepare themselves to become good leaders of men and of their country with a strong motivation to strive for excellence and shun mediocrity in all things. They promised to devote themselves to the service of their country.

This group of 5 brought about a unity of purpose untold and even though school boys at the time, they continued to follow this inspiring Constitution till death.. Further God's Leaders Squad spread to many schools in India and to date there are more than 120 groups or more scattered throughout India and Nepal. The name was changed to Leadership Training Service in 1965. .

Some of the goals of LTS (Leadership Training Service) which have been carried out during the past 52 years or more are: Intellectual formation, service to the country and fellowmen especially the poor, patriotism, excellence and future leadership in business and the country. The motto chosen was and is "For God and Country-so let your light shine"

The following is what Vinoba Bhave , a great leader in India said to the Founder in April 1961 (courtesy Back to the Roots: LTS Pub)

"What India and the whole world need today are good spiritual and intellectual leaders...

Tell your boys to be good leaders to aspire to high ideals and above all to love God and their country and also never to underestimate the goodwill of the people. Tell them that the age is with them. There is no time to lose. Now is the time for action."

It is with deep gratitude and praise that I recall that the LTS has proved to be a wonderful movement for youth of `all nationalities, religions and cultures, who have taken their foundations seriously. Many have served the Country (India) in various ways, even

in Government. Others have moved to foreign lands, where they live their principles and values in their family and work. Several are in US in specialized jobs and a number of them are in Canada, living out their values and integrating into a multi-colored society with leadership of service.

You ask me how I know this:. Well I was the National Promoter of this movement for 12 years in India. (Do check out LTS on Facebook and enjoy what they are doing to make a better world),

> For God , our Country and our World, let your light shine regardless of religion, culture , language ....let there be unity in diversity because those are the multi-colored flowers of the world..

PETALS FROM THE MULTI-COLORED FLOWER

CLAYPOTS!! WE ARE ONE IN THE SPIRIT

Imagine a number of clay pots being fashioned in different patterns by the Potter. They have different names, forms, shapes and colors, according to the purpose they are to fulfil in life. Yet all of them are ONE, because they are made of the same stuff..clay..without which none of these pots exist. From clay they came, in clay they exist and when they cease to exist, their names, forms, shapes and colors all merge into ONE..clay. However, there is a fusion of all these clay pots in the Vision and Spirit of their Creator, the Potter. This clay apparently lifeless, takes form and purpose from its Potter and because of this there is UNITY and fusion into a 'whole'...a ONENESS in a Spirit that NEVER DIES.

I am sure this example expresses fully a theme. It speaks to us of the whole world with its similarities and differences. We are all products of one Potter, our Creator, and though different in form, shape, color, religion, it is only when we are united in Him, the Spirit, the' Atma', that we can become ONE, without losing our uniqueness and identity.

This Spirit not only creates the 'clay pots' giving them life, but harmonizes their existence with the Universe and with each other.

The Spirit of God reveals himself everywhere because he is the ultimate point upon which all creation converges. It is when we fulfil the purpose for which we are created that we can harmonize with Him-this is what doing His Will means concretely.

This theme 'One in the Spirit' confronts us in our reality which today is quite opposite to harmony. What then are those elements that prevent us from unity and harmony when we are all basically one?

Disintegration and disunity stems from three evils: Greed, Lust and Pride. It is man's Greed for more and more things, his Lust for Power and his Vanity that makes him disintegrated within himself and this interferes with the purpose of others' lives. This separates man from the Spirit of God and therefore from harmony and unity. To really live this theme today, we need to

(1) Bring harmony within ourselves. It is the battle of the EGO vs True Self. Ego focuses on self and its greed , lust and vanity.

> True Self focuses on God and others and one's own gifts and
>
> uniqueness which are to be used in service to humanity. Ask
>
> yourself who you are and who you are trying to be? Is there
>
> harmony in that?

(2) Are you in touch with your Centre? Is it the Spirit of God,

> ambition or self?

(3) Are you helping others pursue their God-given purpose in life,

> or are you diverting them with your possessiveness, domination,
>
> negative attitude and others?

Let us all evaluate our dispositions and attitudes so that we may start the process to harmony and unity, with ALL PEOPLES in our country and the world in ONE SPIRIT, for in this is PEACE.

PETALS OF THE MULTI-COLORED FLOWER

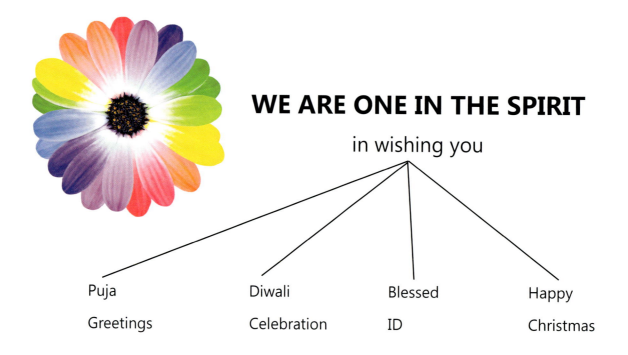

WE ARE ONE IN THE SPIRIT

in wishing you

Puja Greetings | Diwali Celebration | Blessed ID | Happy Christmas

Reflecting on the festivals we celebrate each year, one is struck with the harmony that exists between them. For instance, the pujas bring us the realization that good overpowers evil. Diwali brings us 'light', ID reminds us that sacrifice is necessary to God and Christmas brings us this "living sacrifice" in human form as the Light which overcomes the darkness of evil for all mankind.

Perhaps when we look back on the past months, we realize that the world is in a momentum of 'change' but change without God's touch means very little 'change of heart'. On the contrary change is going to the other extreme. This, I feel is a danger for, as we all know, if batteries are put into a torch with two negative points touching, it will not light. We are still left in darkness.

2/

In East and West too change is there, but from facts and experiences, it seems to be going 'negative' just now. The rule of the fittest, the rod of the strongest, the 'roll' of the rich and the rake of the exploiter are, it would seem, in full swing!

A feeling of human insecurity prevails in all walks of life.

A young man once told me."We have tried everything, now we must give God a chance"

However the vital question is 'what kind of God?'

Is he the kind which people invent during these festive seasons in the way they behave, in the way they spend and waste. He may be just an 'excuse' for many, a salve for their troubled minds. He may be also a 'god' who is only available to one caste, one creed or even a god of lesser people! Or is he a walkie/talkie god who does and says what you want him to. So inherent is our single-minded ego, that we all invent our 'own' god and when he does not do what we wish, some say

'there is no god'…..it is the utter illogicality of the human reality!

As people today we ought to be very sure of the God we believe in since he is our Leader, Creator and Father. How else then does 'serving' humanity become our endeavour? It is because of the fact that God, our Father, makes us all brothers and sisters.

Giving God a chance, I mean, Creator Father and Leader will make a difference. Of course this doesn't mean sitting back but rather a collaboration by spreading His message, available in all 'authentic' scripture, spreading values of the dignity of the human person, non-violence, truth and peace.

As we journey through our festivals from year to year let us give thought to what may lead us to 'concrete' action as individuals and human community for positive change in the society at large.

Let us do some spring cleaning and open the windows of our soul to fresh air and sunlight.

....

WE ARE ONE IN THE SPIRIT : IN ACTION

I had the most extraordinary experience with a family who had eight children. The family was Hindu. A gentleman came to our house and said: "Mother Teresa, there is a family of eight children: they have not eaten for so long; do something" So I took some rice and went there immediately. I saw the children-their eyes shining with hunger. I don't know if you have ever seen hunger. But I have seen it very often. And she took the rice, she divided the rice and went out. When she came back I asked her "Where did you go, what did you do?" And she gave me a very simple answer: " They are hungry also". What struck me most was that she knew who they are…. A Muslim family- and she knew . I didn't bring more rice that evening because I wanted them to enjoy the Joy of Sharing.

But there were these children, radiating joy, sharing the joy with their mother because she had the love to give. And you see this where love begins-at home.

(Extract from Mother Teresa's acceptance speech given at Oslo, Norway in 1979 on the occasion of Nobel Peace Prize)   (715 words)

PETALS OF GOLD

LIVE THE GOLDEN RULE AND BE ALL THAT YOU CAN BE TO HELP MAKE THIS A BETTER WORLD WHEREVER YOU ARE.

WHAT IS THE GOLDEN RULE?

This golden rule is a familiar ethical principle in many cultures. We also find variations of it in different spiritual traditions.

"DO UNTO OTHERS AS YOU WOULD HAVE THEM DO UNTO YOU"

Buddhists say: Hurt not others in ways that you yourself would find hurtful. The words are different but the meaning is the same.

Confucianism: Is there one maxim which ought to be acted upon throughout one's whole life? Surely it is the maxim of loving kindness: Do not unto others what you would not have them do unto you (Analects 15: 23)

Hinduism: This is the sum of duty: do naught unto others which would cause you pain if done to you (Mahabharata 5:15-17)

Islam: No one of you is a believer until he desires for his brother that which he desires for himself (Sunnah)

Judaism: What is hateful to you, do not to your fellowmen. This is the entire Law; all the rest is commentary (Talmud, Shabbat 3id)

Taoism: Regard your neighbor's gain as your own gain, and your neighbor's loss as your own loss (Tai Shang Kan Ving P'ien)

When the Golden Rule is put into practice the world becomes a better and happier place to live in because society is in order and you yourself become an attractive and charming person. Politeness, civility and human warmth are always responded to instantly.

There are 9 personality points to work on to practice the Golden Rule

1. Show genuine appreciation:

    Do you like to be thanked? Then say a 'thank you' to others

2. Give compliments:

    Truthful praise brings joy to anyone's life. Little compliments can pay big dividends.

3. Point out the good in others:

    Let others know that you see good things in them.

4. Follow generous impulses: As you like to be warmly accepted, look for ways of welcoming others.

5. Develop tolerance and respect.

    Just as you want others to respect you, show respect to them even when it is hard. Remember to show respect to the old and infirm as well

6. Practice kindness:

    This is the attitude of mind which welcomes strangers as family especially try to make the old people feel wanted, not only in your family but in buses and the marketplace.

7. Ease the burden of others:

    By forgiving others their mistakes you ease them and help them to start anew. Ease the burdens of the sick and aged by bringing them your warmth through a visit, a card or a telephone call.

8. Act cheerfully. Ordinary hardships of life come and go, try and accept them in a cheerful manner.

9. Learn how to smile: A smile is one of the nicest gifts you can give. A winning smile can make a face beautiful.

'Smile a little, smile a little
Be for earth a leaven
And perhaps you'll give another
Just a little glimpse of heaven'
(John Jarvis)

ILLUSION vs REALITY

When religion is seen outside the person, only in rallies, processions, temples, churches, mosques, in giving donations for popularity, it can be said that this type of religion is illusion, without a proper reason and purpose.

All religions and especially those of one's sacred heritage have one primary concern and that is to help and guide humans to experience God in self-realization in the Divine and this is always through the REALITY of our relationships and the universe. If my brother or sister suffers, then God suffers in them and I must respond to help.

In the Hindu religion the idea of Dharma is a development of rta, which means "cosmic and moral order"

"Dharma is the state of being held together , the reality of cosmic integration. Dharma is the dynamics of historical process and the motivation for ethical life. Dharma is the experience of God leading all to the final fulfilment." (ref.Dharmasasamsthapanam Gita, 4: 8; 14: 27; 18: 66).

Therefore we ask the question

How then does any religion take to violence amd communal negativism and proclaim that it is fulfilling the goal of life and the path to peace and harmony i.e. Dharma? Is this not ILLUSION of the meanest order?

The writing of this piece is to make people aware of the ILLUSION of fanatic religion which is neither God-centered or People oriented.

Become aware of the REALITY that religion must transform the heart , must help us build temples within, in our values and attitudes and our relationships to one another.

Some readers may remember reading the mythical story in the Gita when Krishna spent a long time trying to help Arjuna change his attitudes first. The battle of the Mahabharata is within, not without. It is the battle within the inner selves from which comes both good and evil.

For us in this century it is a great consolation and surely a God-given blessing to sit together and pray to ONE GOD for all those interreligious gatherings . Spread the REALITY of religion and not the ILLUSION to your family and friends. We hope that good-minded people build integration in love, truth and freedom.

Here are some practical ways:

-After reading this article, what feelings does it invoke in you?

-Do you agree with the ideas...why....why not?

-How can you build integration in love, truth and freedom.

A PARODOX..........?

WHICH END OF THE ROPE ARE YOU HOLDING?

It is a fact of life that there are two ends to everything. For instance, if you overdo something in life, it's opposite or polarity will appear.

A person who is obsessed with being beautiful turns out to be ugly , and one obsessed with success becomes unsuccessful. Obsessed with money one becomes 'poor' and obsessed with being a leader eventually becomes a follower in the 'last line'!

All wise people throughout the ages have understood too well the paradox of polarities while they were growing up in facing situations in life.

WHICH END OF THE ROPE ARE YOU HOLDING READER?

Are you , for example, overdoing 'leadership' and thereby compromising on values and behaviour? Power games, manipulating others and vying for position and fame, have colored motivation, breeding disunity and disharmony which indicate that you are clutching the polarity or wrong end of the rope.

We were all shocked to see the body of young baby boy lying on the beach, cold dead but what about the thousands of aborted babies who lie dissected with body parts sold for a profit!! Which end of the rope is this?

May I encourage you to stop and reflect on which end of the rope you are clutching now in life. A wise person does not push or manipulate to make things happen, but allows an unfolding of events. A wise person teaches by example, rather than 'long talk'. He/she does not block others in the group by constantly taking over and having things his/her own way.

A wise person forgives and rebuilds on disagreements and ensures peace and harmony.

Face yourself on the polarity you have chosen...is it undoing the very purpose of your being as a person. You may or may not be aware of the end of the rope you are clutching. Just STOP- LOOK - LISTEN - CHANGE AND GO!

VIRTUES AND VALUES

It is true that over the years Virtues and Character Development have been lost in our vocabulary and maybe in education as well. This has led to emphasis on 'personality' only, not character development...after all personality outside ought to be a reflection of what is inside!

I would like to amplify on virtues and values.

Virtues are many coming from our religious beliefs and from role models, be they parents, teachers, grandparents and even very ordinary people. In the last 20 years or so there has been a dearth of role models of value or virtue rather there have been role models of fashion, violence, hype and so on.

For virtues to be imbibed one needs values as well. What is a value?

-It is something one chooses from alternatives. Example : if the virtue is truth then one chooses truth and puts aside untruth.

-Virtue to be a value must be freely chosen, not imposed and so one needs to know what the virtue will do to make one a better person.

-Virtue needs to be practised frequently so it becomes a value(a treasure) to be cherished.

-One needs to affirm the virtue as a value when the person stands up for it publicly..the person is known or recognised by that value /virtue.

What I am advocating is that just propagating virtues will not help bring transformation and character development. Those virtues need to be accepted as values, as treasures, by which a person lives.

_____

INNER FREEDOM AND INTEGRITY

The key to peace in this world and in one's country is 'inner freedom and integrity'.

We keep yearning constantly for freedom and liberation and sometimes are blissfully unaware of our slavery. Slavery by which we chain ourselves and slavery imposed on us and which we accept.

Rabindranath Tagore in his poem in 'Gitanjali' asks:

"Prisoner tell me, who was it that wrought this

unbreakable chain?" "It was I", said the prisoner, 'who

forged this chain very carefully, I thought my invincible

power would hold the world captive leaving me in a

freedom undisturbed....Thus night and day I worked at the

chain with huge fires and cruel hard strokes. When at last

the work was done and the links were complete and   unbreakable, I found that it held me in its grip." (XXXI)

To strive for inner freedom and integrity is a life long quest, for the more we attain inner freedom, the more we realize that there are many areas in which we are slaves to our own selfishness, self-image and the image others have of us to our pride, our greed for fame and wealth.

Inner freedom and integrity is thus gained in the measure of our struggle in these areas so that we become truly and wholly free.

Inner freedom and integrity are gained by having a God-nonomous life ..one pervaded by His Spirit of Truth and Love.

Some areas of struggle come to mind for young people who are

aspiring to be leaders and integrated persons.

CONDITIONING by others, perhaps your own peer group. Your fear of being left out makes you accept the slavery others impose on you.

INTELLECTUAL PRIDE: the attitude that you know more than others and what you say is the only way. Not able to take genuine correction either.

EGO/ONEUPMANSHIP: always showing that you can do more and better than others and if you are not around, things are not so good.

GOSSIPING: ….the urge to create sensation in order to show up other people.

These are some forms of slavery to which young people and people in general conform. However, each one has the 'power of freedom'…it is a power and it is God-given and within you.

YOUR POWER OF CHOICE

Your power of choice based on integrity and responsibility, is something no one can take away. Freedom is a beautiful gift because freedom means a relationship of love and God has given us freedom because He loves each one. However, people today are forced to exchange freedom for many forms of domination and manipulation. You can see this in the deprived and poor around us. Sometimes your freedom gets "hijacked" by cable TV, films, advertisements and technology and so you give away your 'power of choice' and become one of the crowd.

Freedom means responsibility in exercising your power of choice which is built on two fundamental and absolute values which give integrity i.e.

God is our Creator and Father and we are all brothers and sisters

You, young people, are in a very important stage of growth in personal freedom but somehow your growth is uneven. Your rapid growth in freedom is not balanced with your willingness to take responsibility. This is a contradiction all of you are facing as young people. However as 'Petals of the Multi-Colored Flower', who in the story brought about integration and harmony, you are bound to balance personal freedom with personal responsibility in using that freedom in small and big events. This leads to self-direction instead of short-sightedness when you are unable to see the full implications of your actions.

BUILD BRIDGES NOT WALLS

In times of war, the enemy sights strategic points for destruction and one of these is a bridge or bridges. Why is this? Because bridges link people, transport items for daily living and connect lands ...a bridge means fostering 'Life'.

In blowing up bridges, vital communications are destroyed and people isolated and alienated. They are confined to their own 'walls'.

There was great JOY when the Berlin Wall came down and links were restored between peoples of the same race, previously walled in and divided for so many years.

Build Bridges not Walls is the way to build the Multi-Colored Flower and here are some thoughts to further explore this theme in terms of active responses in the family, neighbourhood and country.

Building Bridges is got to do with building relationships, not just with friends but with 'foes'..people we don't like, people different from us and therefore it calls for a whole lot of acceptance and interaction. Frequently we hear 'Why do I need other people, why not have our own gang'?

Sometimes one comes across an experience where people in society want to know where you have originally come from and on this basis one is included or excluded. This has been my experience but it only challenges me to go out and enter into the company of those who seem to exclude. Exclusion is the Wall I am referring to and in society this is the norm.....a car, a house, bank accounts make you one to be included!! A Wall is built in relationships when there are prejudices, unhealthy competition, clever winning strategies which bring us what we want , regardless of others.

A time for building bridges is now because the world is so impoverished by lack of human dignity and the culture of death.

The bridges I am referring to are encouraging and living out the virtues and values of Loving, Healing, Forgiving Renewing, Reconciling, Planting, Sowing and Growing. These bridges are the QUALITY of our relationships.

You can be a 'bridge over troubled waters' too in your family, school, neighbourhood. You young people have already started building bridges in small ways and you are to be congratulated. However you are called to build as part of the Master Bridge, the one on which all bridges are patterned.

Do we need more temples, churches or mosques? We need bridges of human relationships when each one can call the other Brother/Sister/Father/Mother….And so each one shares and gives to the other for this is the meaning of Life and Living.

You, young people , can make this happen , you are the multi-colored petal helping to put all together to make that multi-colored flower of people united and sharing.

BUILD BRIDGES NOT WALLS

Take up the stone of yourself and with chisel, hammer and clay of determination and effort lay yourself down to be a Bridge…..the Time is Now and Response is Urgent.

BUILD BRIDGES WITH A FOUNTAIN OF JOY

Building bridges is always a Challenge but it is something you will enjoy. A bridge cannot choose its travellers but must be open to all people…poor, rich, black, white, this religion or that. A bridge is solid in its foundations which gets washed day and

night by the water. A bridge is a very integrated structure..well-balanced, otherwise it would not stand. So also is each one who strives for integration and balance.

Do this and Be Happy. A bridge does not groan or moan though it may squeak sometimes. Refrain from complaining and comparing.

Being Happy means acceptance of Self, Situations and Others.

There is a formula for Happiness given to us by John Powell sj

$H = IJ$:   Happiness equals Inside Job

If things outside you make you happy it will not last and you will want more and more of the same. The INSIDE JOB means things you work on and clarify for yourself like

The meaning of life

Acceptance of yourself and others

Values

Service

If these inside tapes are clarified then happiness is yours and you become a Bridge and a Joyful one at that.

MULTICULTURALISM - ASSISSIMILATION TOWARDS INTEGRATION

THE SALAD BOWL

The Salad Bowl is an everyday item on most

Family food tables.

Now think of this: Would you like a salad with the veggies, carrots, tomatoes, cucumbers and more just lined separately in the bowl without any other items

OR

Would you like a Salad with the veggies all mixed together with salad dressing

OR

Still again, would you like a Salad with veggies all mixed together with salad dressing, salad oil and some mustard to add that yummy flavor?

These simple examples describe very well what the title of this page is all about.

Let us go further.

MULTICULTURALISM is like the first salad bowl. Each culture/religion interact in their own groups. Each culture does respect the dominant culture of the country and enjoy the benefits like education, jobs, training. Those who immigrate sometimes do very well if they are accepting of the dominant culture. Most often there is very little sense of belonging.

MULTICULTURALISM is not meant to be as described in the previous paragraph. The original advantages to immigrants and others are very positive. Let us take Canada for example to see some of these positive elements.

-People seem to be more tolerant of other ethnic groups, even today.

-There are better prospects for people from other countries.

-People feel welcomed on the whole.

-There are ideas (and I say ideas) to unite in diversity.

-There is a freedom of speech

-There is a democratic set up

Although these are good, they are mostly in ideas and speeches.

In reality today 2015, people are not united.

More and more they tend to interact in their own cultural and religious groups

Another factor is that those immigrants who are educated and grow up in Canada absorb the culture of the country. They lose the culture of their original birthplace

which causes many family feuds and even violence.

On the other hand, older immigrants tend not to make any effort to absorb the culture in its positive values and so this leads to alienation and resentment. This then develops into hate crimes.

The younger generation feel the deprivation of inclusion into the society and always have the notion that they are 'second-class'.

So they make it a point to prove this over and over again in protests, gun wars with police and in other violent ways.

So we can conclude from this that the whole idea of MULTICULTURALISM as practised in some western countries is not leading to what is positive unity in diversity.

I must say language is a great barrier to MULTICULTURALISM.

What then is ASSISIMILATION?

It is like the second Salad Bowl...a good mix of everything with salad dressing!

ASSISIMILATION is a process where members of ethno-cultural groups are "mixed" into one dominant community. Each one is one single identity emerging into the melting pot. And this mixed community is a power house for the whole world.

The example of America fits this description. Something is missing in this salad..... something with a touch of 'flavor'

Let us see how America has benefitted or not from this process.

Advantages: people are more unified, especially in time of crisis, there is an increased standard of living for immigrants as well. Indigenous people have been given the necessary education and training to make it good.

Disadvantages: People seem to be less tolerant of other ethnic groups. English is made compulsory and this is not accepted by some. In the fast moving system of America, people are expected to shed their own culture and even religion. The assimilated group loses many cultural ways by being absorbed in the one culture.

Government does not recognize different kinds of groups.

Here again there is that second class mentality on both sides and leads to resentment, anger, revenge and all the disvalues you can think of.

Though MULTICULTURALISM and ASSISIMILATION both have their advantages and disadvantages and in some cases have proved good to immigrants and others, could there be a third way, like the third Salad Bowl with oil, dressing and the best of mustard giving a flavor.

INTEGRATION: What is INTEGRATION?

It is what brings us back to 'Basics'

It calls for the quality of person and the quality of that person's rapport with others and nature. (Rene Cortazar).

INTEGRATION is making a complete whole by adding parts and bringing them into the dominant society as equals. It moves to desegregate especially racially. It includes not excludes!

This is not to say that communities with their culture need to lose their identity altogether. No, they keep their culture, religion and style without imposing these on anyone. Instead they share aspects of their communities with the other communities. One might ask how this is achieved. Well, the keyword is SHARING.

This brings into focus the story of the multi-colored flower. The young seeds told the gardener of their plan: "While we wish to be ourselves roses, lilies and so on, we want to give a petal or two each to form a multi-colored flower which will remind us that we are one and united" What a flavor this gives to the whole matter.

You might ask how does one do this type of sharing . Well if you look round it has already started, though it needs more strengthening.

In which areas can INTEGRATION take place through sharing. Definitely the Arts lend themselves to this sharing. The different ethnic groups can SHARE music, skills, literature, fashion, technology, artistic ventures, culinary delights and dance forms not to forget languages.

This type of INTEGRATION will bring people closer and united. Working in segregated groups and pockets leads to rivalry in most cases. Sharing leads to relationships and unity in diversity.

No culture on earth is perfect or fully integrated. However, every culture has a soul that gives it life and meaning and this is what must be brought back to play in order to build a multi-cultural society with a flavor that speaks sharing and therefore peace truly integrated as a people, as a nation.

Edwards Brothers Malloy
Ann Arbor MI. USA
July 14, 2017